TRUCK

Donald Crews

Library of Congress Cataloging in Publication Data
Crews, Donald. Truck. [1. Trucks–Pictorial works.
2. Stories without words] I. Title. PZ7. C8682Tr
[E] 79-19031 ISBN 978-0-688-80244-8
ISBN 978-0-688-84244-4 lib. bdg. ISBN 978-0-688-10481-8 pbk.

The art was prepared in four halftone separations
combined with black line drawings.

To A/N/A/D/J/M and especially Malcolm

Greenwillow Books/New York

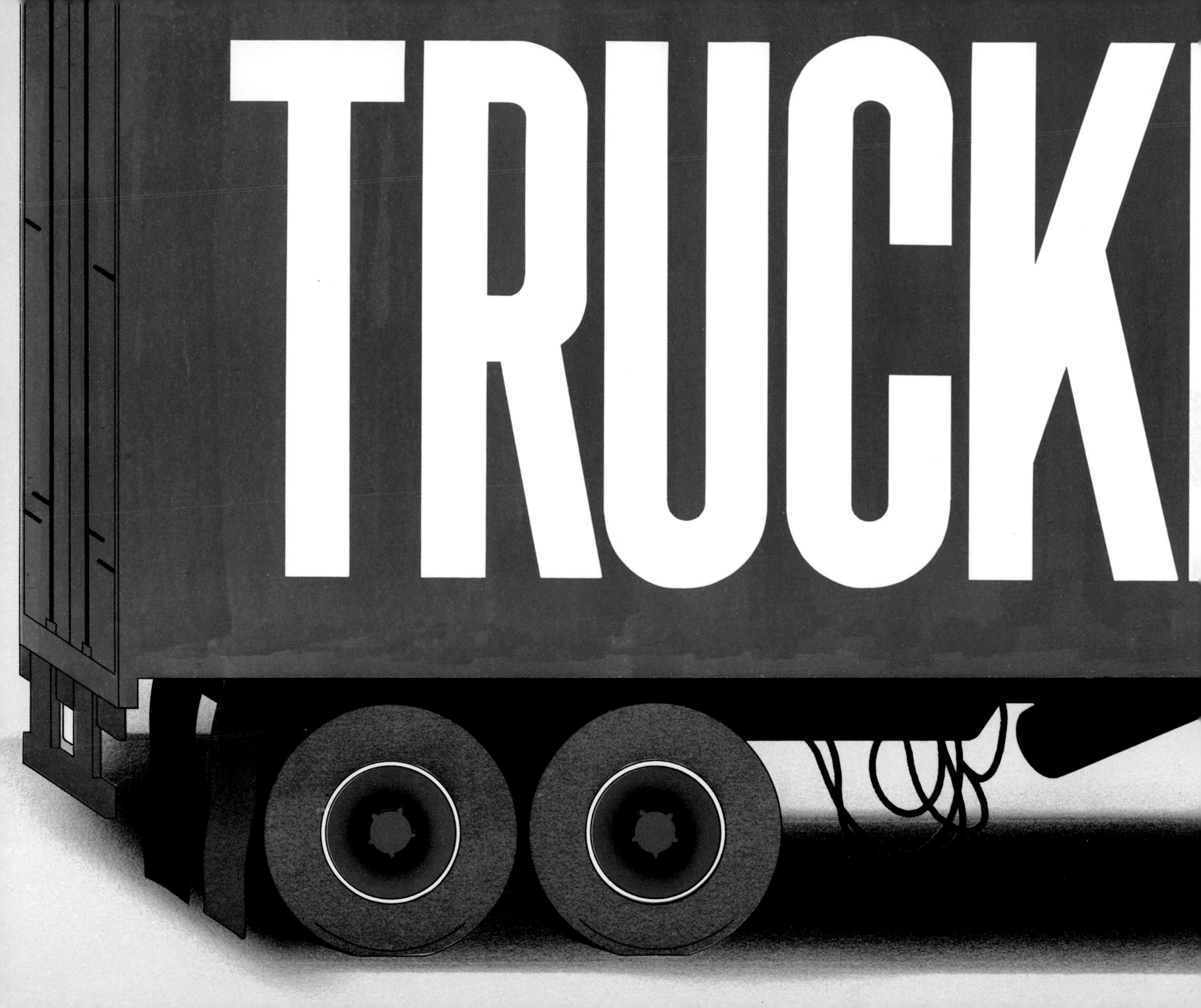
TRUCK

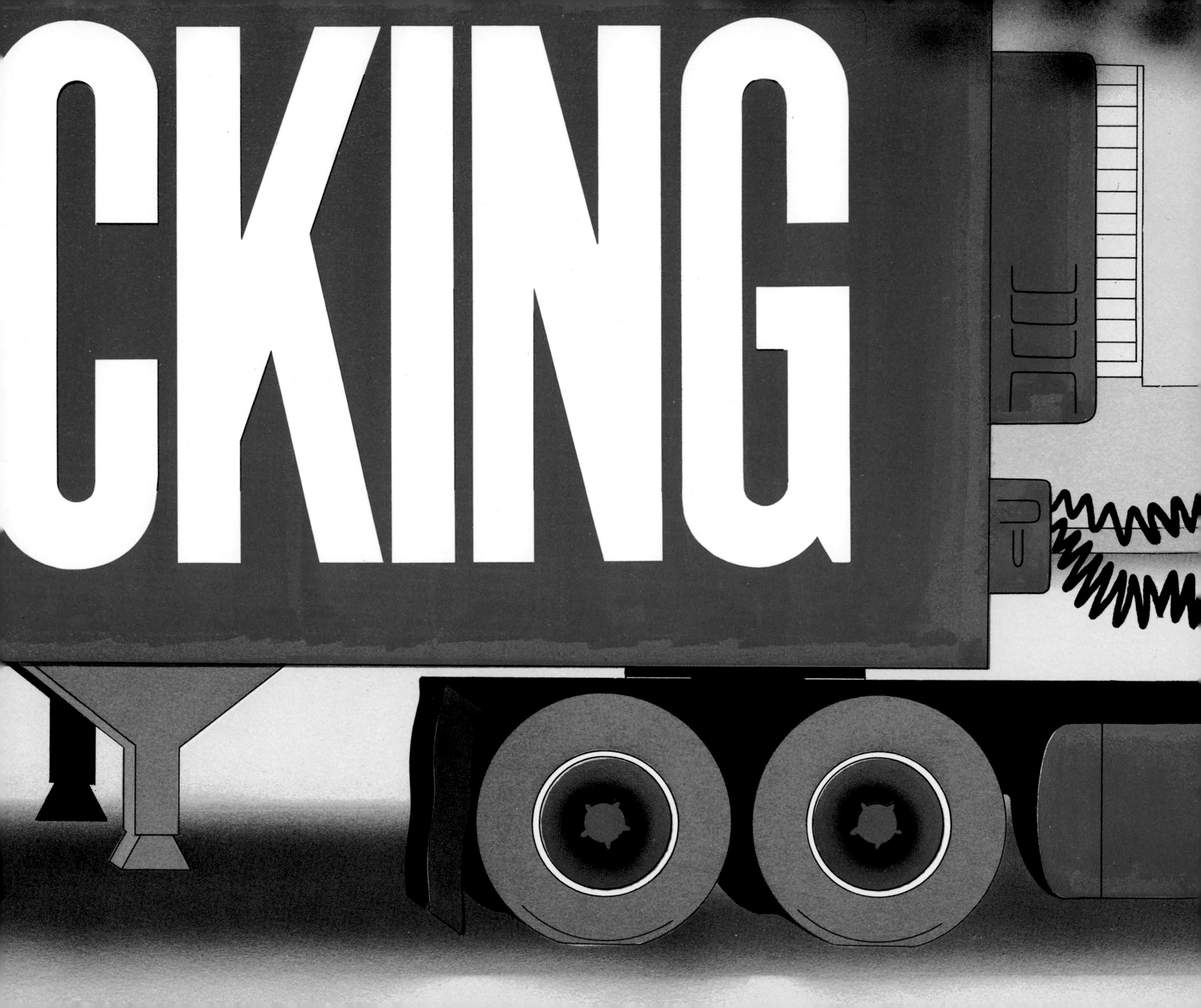
CKING

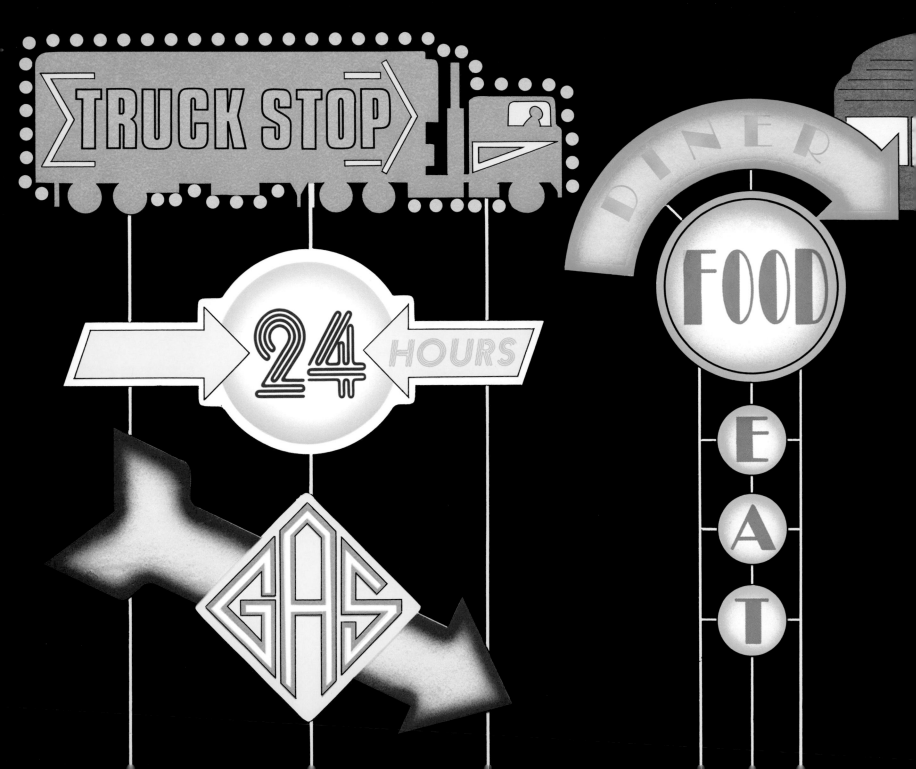

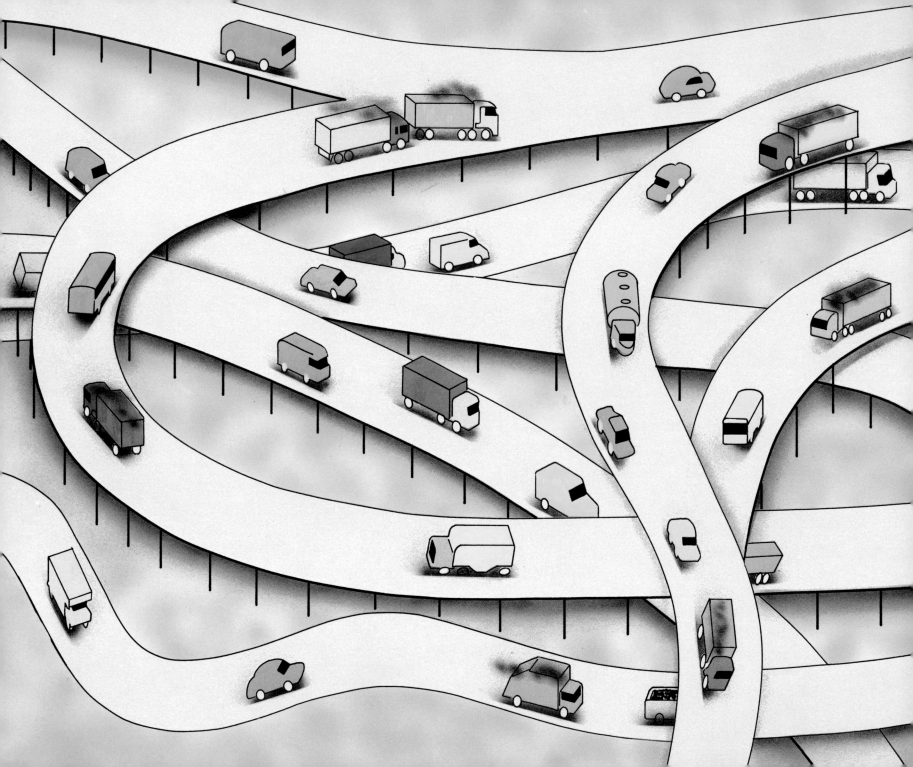

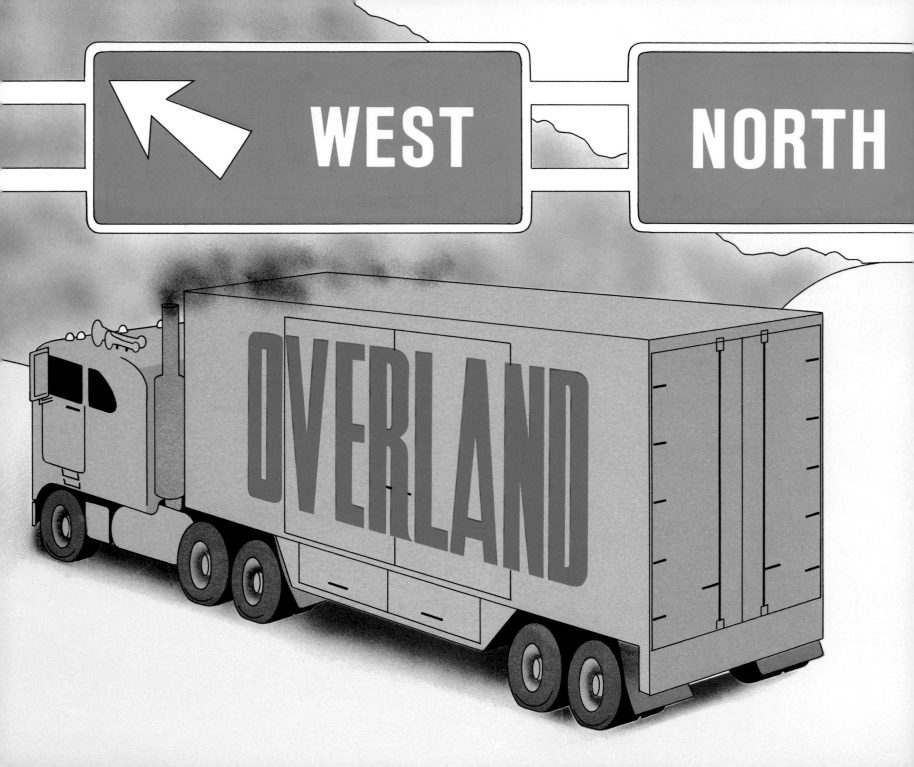